AF604779

Growing up Wiradjuri

Stories from the Wiradjuri Nation

Edited by
Dr Anita Heiss

This is a Magabala Book

LEADING PUBLISHER OF ABORIGINAL AND
TORRES STRAIT ISLANDER STORYTELLERS.

CHANGING THE WORLD, ONE STORY AT A TIME.

First published 2022
Magabala Books Aboriginal Corporation
1 Bagot Street, Broome, Western Australia
Website: www.magabala.com
Email: sales@magabala.com

Magabala Books receives financial assistance from the Commonwealth Government through the Australia Council, its arts advisory body. The State of Western Australia has made an investment in this project through the Department of Local Government, Sport and Cultural Industries. Magabala Books would like to acknowledge the support of the Shire of Broome, Western Australia.

Magabala Books is Australia's only independent Aboriginal and Torres Strait Islander publishing house. Magabala Books acknowledges the Traditional Owners of the Country on which we live and work. We recognise the unbroken connection to traditional lands, waters and cultures. Through what we publish, we honour all our Elders, peoples and stories, past, present and future.

Cover Design Gene Eaton, Inland Studios
Typeset by Post Pre-press Group
Cover art by Luke Penrith
Printed and bound by McPherson's Printing Group

ISBN (Print): 978-1-922613-74-5
ISBN (ePDF) 978-1-922613-67-7

Department of
**Local Government, Sport
and Cultural Industries**

Contents

Foreword

Dr Anita Heiss

The *Growing Up Wiradjuri* anthology was born out of a community development project I chose to do as part of my Graduate Certificate in Wiradjuri Language, Culture and Heritage through Charles Sturt University.

That original idea has become a gift to the nation by some of our most treasured Elders, who have generously shared stories that document a range of experiences growing up on and off Wiradjuri Country, in bush camps and on reserves, in country towns, cities and in humpies along riverbanks.

Some of these stories include knowledge and Culture that has been passed down from generation to generation. Some include childhood games of the past, elements of our language almost lost forever, and what our connection to family and Country means to us as Wiradjuri peoples. All of them form part of our collective history, the way we speak of and live Culture still today, and the importance of passing on such stories to younger generations.

Like me, I hope those reading *Growing Up Wiradjuri* also feel proud of the resilience and the strength of Wiradjuri Elders. I hope you realise that we have always worked hard, been able to laugh and have fun, and that we are epic storytellers. I hope this anthology helps you see us the way we see ourselves. As deadly!

From my heart to yours, I say mandaang guwu to Aunties Lorraine, Elaine, Cheryl, Mary and Isabel and Uncles Stan, James and Norman. You have given us so much to be grateful for.

Where Do You Start Being Wiradjuri?

Aunty Lorraine Tye

The first grandparents that I can trace back to were born in the early 1800s. Bridget and John Chisholm gave birth to Caroline in 1838 at Gunning, New South Wales. Caroline married Andy Lane in 1855 at Boorowa. They had six children, the youngest being Lexter. Lexter was born in 1862 at Bowning, New South Wales. Lexter had three children with John Samuel Brown. He was always known as Sam Brown.

Their youngest child is my nan, Zillah. She was born in 1907 at Rye Park, New South Wales. Zillah married my pop, Albert Whittaker Snr, known as Bert, in 1925 at Boorowa. They had nine children, my father Albert Whittaker being the eldest.

Zillah and Bert travelled for work soon after they married. My grandfather Bert was a wanderer, and some of the places they worked at included Wellington, Gooloogong, Yass, Woodstock and Goulburn. They lived in a tent or wagonette on the reserves and Aboriginal camps. In the 1930s they moved to Wagga Wagga.

When they came to Wagga, they stayed the longest they had ever been in a town. They lived in a part of Wagga Wagga that was called 'tin town', that was a small area for Aboriginal and very poor people.

They then moved on to what was known as the island with a Chinese man who worked a market garden. Pop worked for them, and later Dad and Pop took over the market garden. They were still running the garden in 1945 when Mum and Dad were married, although Dad went shearing whenever he had work. I don't know what year they left the island market garden.

My nan died in 1949, she was 43 years old, and Pop left Wagga Wagga in 1950 taking all the younger children with him. In September 1950 he left ten-year-old Pam in the Bathurst Sisters of Mercy Children's Home. He wandered for a while and eventually joined the railway in Wellington.

Dad is a Wiradjuri man. He was born on the Aboriginal reserve at Rye Park, New South Wales, in 1925. Dad stayed in Wagga Wagga to raise his family. Mum was a Wagga girl and wouldn't move. Dad was a shearer, so I suppose he did travel all his life. When my dad passed, he was only 53 years old.

The two youngest girls at the Bathurst Children's Home were being relocated. When Aunty Pam was 15 years old, the home organised a job as a companion to a young girl on a station near Bourke.

From the stories I have heard, Dad and his family didn't have an easy time growing up. They weren't seen as black and they weren't white either, they were the fringe dwellers of the communities they lived in.

I am Lorraine, the youngest of three children, and I was born in 1950. I contracted polio at the age of 21 months and spent three months in isolation at Wagga Base Hospital. From there I was sent to the Royal Far

West Children's Home in Sydney. I spent a lot of my childhood in Sydney, staying there for years at a time. Eventually I came home to stay at the age of 14.

Because of the time I spent on my own growing up, and the way my father grew up, our knowledge of our Aboriginal culture and heritage was interrupted. Dad wouldn't talk about his life, and I never had the chance to ask. Looking back now as I get older and learning more about my Culture, I realise that he did teach us a lot, but we just didn't know it at the time.

I think our Culture is inside you. It is a feeling, a belonging and understanding. I have just found out my grandmother made paper flowers and aprons out of chaff bags to sell. Both my sister and I have always been makers, interested in working to make things with our hands. I'm a weaver still learning the traditional ways, but I do a lot of contemporary pieces using grasses, bark, rope, raffia, wire and cloth.

I have met my dad's first cousins, one is now 98, they grew up with Dad on the reserve where my father was born. They have told me all the family stories that I missed out on growing up.

My passion is now to make sure future generations know and are aware of all the past history of our Culture and traditions. As some Elders say, 'Our Culture is not lost, just waiting to be remembered'.

Many worlds, Many ways,
Through cobwebs of stories
Stringing pathways
Of lives intertwining.

Gadhaang Yiradhu-galang (Happy Days)

Aunty Elaine Lomas

Dedicated to Wormy (16 December 1946 – 12 October 2021), my brother for life. This is a story about him growing up Wiradyuri too.

The rabbit traps jingle-jangled as I walked over one of the many dry, dusty sheep-tracked paddocks in and around Weethalle. Weethalle is near Griffith, on my Wiradyuri ngurambang in south-western New South Wales.

This particular day in early 1957 started out very hot and dry, with no hint of rain in sight. Sometimes a light, cool breeze would give us a spell from the heat and would whip up the dusty paddocks into a giant whirly whirly, causing the dust to get into everyone's eyes and hair.

We spent many weekends and school holidays trapping rabbits for a living in between my uncle's jobs. He and his wife brought me up after my mother died when I was two years old. That's what our old people did in those days to stop the welfare board from taking our kids and sending them to the children's homes.

Everyone was given traps to carry. I was only seven years old, and I was given five traps. My brother was 12, so he carried more, because they were too heavy for both me and my sister. Sometimes we walked and walked for hours, playing as we went along. Our games were simple and fun; sometimes we would see who was the first one to spot a rabbit running around and then count how many we saw and then we would fight over who got the most. Hahaha!

When all of the kids' traps were set, we could run off and play chasies, or we used a stick to draw circles on the ground as we spun around.

Sometimes we would see porcupines, or wandayali,

as our old people called them. Uncle would catch it and kill it, burn off the quills and then cook it in the ashes. It was good eating especially when you were hungry. It tasted like pork, and the wandayali fat dripping from it was yummy or marambang bilang on johnny cakes. We licked our fingers all over to make sure there wasn't any fat left on them.

We used a lot of our language but only easy words like wigay, which meant bread, and dhangaang for food. Wiray for no and ngawa for yes. We knew wirrinya meant sleep, but we knew many other words as well.

Our best part of the day was when all the traps were set and we could go back to our ngurang, our camp, that Uncle and my big brother had built. We always tried to build our ngurang near a dam, a billabong or creek where we had galing to drink.

We needed a place to wash ourselves as well. Me and my brother and our big sister would love to jump in the water to cool ourselves down too. We would swim around until our feet touched something scary and we would jump out real quick, scared in case it was a gudi. That's a snake or a bunyip; the scary underwater creature that took kids into his watery hole and kept them there never to be seen again.

We were so excited about our ngurang. The best thing was that they had built a two-storey bush hut with us kids sleeping upstairs where we could see the stars through our leafy roof, and underneath was where we ate our meals. Aunty was the best cook. Whatever she made, it always tasted so good.

It was the best bush camp ever, made from bushes and big branches cut from the gum trees. Sometimes, when we would sit around the campfire, we would throw our leftover scraps into the fire. Aunty would tell us not to do that because we were feeding the devil.

Other times we would poke the fire with a stick and wait until the tip caught fire. Then we would take it out and spin it around to make twirly rings or spinning wheels like we had on cracker night. Uncle would tell us not to play with fire as it was making the devil angry. This scared us; we didn't want to upset the devil so we stopped and took our fire sticks and threw them into the fire, hoping he would not be angry with us.

If we drew on the ground with long sticks as the sun was setting, we were told not to do that either because the spirits were going to sleep, and they would be angry if they were disturbed.

After dinner, Uncle would read us from the Bible, then we would sit by the fire and he told us stories at night. The scariest thing that he told us though was about the big mirriyulla dog; he had big red eyes and was often creeping around campfires checking out if there were kids he could take. Us kids would all huddle together at night when we were sleeping, and because I was the youngest, I was always in the middle of the bed. Yay!

We were also told about the little yuriman or hairy man who would come to get us if we were bad or naughty and take us away. Sometimes out in the bush at night when the wind would cause the leaves to make a rustling sound, we would hold our breath thinking it was the little yuriman, or the mirriyulla dog. We would lay there and cling to each other with our eyes closed so we wouldn't see him.

My brother would sing out, 'Dad, what's that noise? Is that the mirriyulla dawg or the yuriman? Dad?'

We were so happy when we were told, 'No, it's just the wind. Go wirrinya now.'

I remember one night when we went to Condobolin to see our mob, we were staying at our other aunty's place on Willow Bend Mission. I was only five or six years old and I needed to go to the toilet which was way, way down the back yard. My sister and cousin woke up to take me, and we stopped where the light finished and the darkness started. I was going to the toilet and I felt something touch my bubul. I looked around and saw this big thing with red eyes. I jumped up and screamed.

'Aunty, mirriyulla dawg! Mirriyulla dawg!'

Aunty hugged me and said, 'No baby it's not a mirriyulla dawg, it's a cow, they live in our back yard.'

I wouldn't believe her but the next morning when I saw the cows, I felt safe that it wasn't the big red-eyed dawg.

We didn't have toys like my white friends. They had dolls and toy cars, toy farmyard animals and cubby houses. But that didn't worry us too much because we were happy. We made our own toys out of branches or old wood laying around, like swords and pretend magic wands. We used empty milk tins and string to make walkie talkies, or we filled them with dirt and put wire through the holes in the top and the bottom and make steam rollers. We would play shops and make mud pies to sell. We used broken glass bottles and bottle tops as money or to play hopscotch. We had real animals too, like Towser our mirri, our dog, and baby rabbits, so soft and snuggly.

What I loved the most about living in the bush was the different smells like the wiiny, the fire and the burning pine and gum leaves with the gentle wafting scent of eucalyptus, especially when the billy can was boiling. My aunty would throw a handful of tea leaves as well as some fresh eucalyptus leaves into the boiling hot water, then when it had finished boiling my big brother would take it off the hook over the fire and swing it around five times one way, then five times the other way, then they would let it settle before pouring it into our jam tin mugs with the lid turned back to make a handle. We added some sugar and a few spoonfuls of our favourite Sunshine Powdered Milk.

We ate johnny cakes with some curried rabbit on it, and our sweets were simply the best: boiled golden syrup dumplings. We'd go off to bed with a full binydyi and we thought we were in heaven.

One day when we went out trapping, we had eaten all the food and we were hoping we could catch a few rabbits or a girawu (a goanna) and a wandayali. We had just about finished setting all the traps. I was feeling so hungry, so I thought I would help the rabbits come out of their burrows and run into the traps. I got the biggest, longest stick and poked it down the last burrow. A big girawu came out and ran up my stick and onto my shoulder. I ran away screaming with that girawu on my shoulder, and my brother was standing there laughing at me. Next thing, the girawu jumped off my shoulder onto his, he took off crying and screaming as well. Uncle, his father, ran to catch him and knocked the girawu off his shoulder. Well, we didn't have rabbit for tea that night, but we had a big girawu with potatoes and damper all cooked in the ashes. What a feed that was.

This story is one of my wonderful memories about growing up Wiradyuri, and something that will never leave me. I have told my kids this story that will be passed down to my grandchildren, mandhaang guwu for listening.

Growing Up Wiradjuri

Aunty Cheryl Penrith

My name is Cheryl Penrith, and when I think about growing up Wiradjuri it takes me to a place I spent the first seven years of my life, Bridge Road, Brungle via Gundagai. The postcode is 2722, the same as Gundagai. Brungle is where my life journey started, in a tin hut built with found materials, a dirt floor, walls pasted with magazines and newspaper, and kerosene lamps on the banks of the Nimbo Creek. We lived just up from the bridge where the Nimbo runs into the Tumut River. It was a magical place to play, with a dog named Sailor, our grandparents and family and a fig tree that is still there today.

My world revolved around my grandmother Emma May Penrith, the boss of our family. She cooked, she made tea in a billy can and she would mix milk and sugar in a cup and dunk it into the tea.

Nan was a beautiful dresser. She was an early riser and always had a scarf on her head, an apron and beautiful jewellery. Nan had polio and when I was little it wasn't so noticeable, but as she grew older it made it hard to get around. Eventually she was in a wheelchair.

Nan told me stories of when she went 'into service', when she was sent away by the Aboriginal Protection Board to become a domestic servant. Nan told me she worked in a bank in Coogee, not as a teller but as the cleaner who got up every day at 5am to clean, dust, mop and polish the whole bank inside and out. It's hard to imagine the life Nan had away from her family and her home, in a big city far away from Brungle.

I used to sleep with Nan and listened to what she had to tell me. If she was tired she would tell me a quick story, but if she wanted to talk she would tell me some amazing stories. She was a knowledge holder and a storyteller, and she told me many things, lots that I could share freely but some that was only for me. Nan told me some magical stories: of spirits, bushrangers, hawkers, of the headless horseman of Killimicat, the fire-breathing dog that was on Brungle mission and the Bunyip that lived in the creek. She told me really special personal stories. I tell those stories to my grandchildren, and they know them off by heart.

Nan was a mail order customer of David Jones for over 40 years, she bought birthday presents and Christmas presents from them. I would go through the catalogue, turning down a corner of a page with things I liked. My favourites were purple jeans with faded purple pockets, very on trend for 1970. At Christmas time she would get a beautiful hamper of luxury food that we would wait all year for.

My nan taught me so many life experiences and lessons. She picked me from a young age and prepared me for leadership of our family and community. She told me who I was related to by blood, but she also told me who to own as family. She told me stories that connected people to place, explained relationships and told me who and what was important to her. Nan was a great lady who was left a legacy five generations and counting. Nan had some interesting sayings too. She would say 'what do people think this is, bush week?', and when you would ask her what was for supper she would say 'bread and fat and swing on the gate'.

Nan was a great storyteller as well as a poet, and she wrote a poem about Brungle Creek. She was a traveller. Usually she'd go to the South Coast. In the early days, she would arrange for one of my uncles to take her and she would always sit in the back with a blanket over her legs. Her port would be put in the boot, and I had to come out and wave goodbye to her. But nearly every time the car was pulling away, I would chase the car and scream and cry for Nan to take me with her, until the brake lights would come on and I jumped in with whatever I had on. Nan would buy me clothes at St Vinnie's along the road. On our way to the coast, we always stopped for a feed at Fitzroy Falls, we would stop at Moss Vale and get bread at Devon and a few chips. We always travelled with a billy can to make tea and mugs and tea leaves and this spot at Fitzroy Falls had a fireplace and wood so you could put the billy on, have a warm and a feed, and my uncle could have a rest before we went down the mountain. We would be sitting there and there would be noise out in the bush, maybe the echo of a whip cracking, Nan would say, 'Hear that, Cheryl? That's not a whip cracking!' She told me there was a hairy man that lived in these mountains that mimicked the sounds of things like a siren going off, a baby crying, chopping wood and whips cracking. She said to me, 'Don't be fooled by them sounds, they are to coax people out into the bush. Stay on the path you are on and don't be distracted, that's no whip cracking Cheryl. That's the dhulagharl.' It always made a shiver go up my spine, and I would hold onto Nanny.

Our times travelling were the best. She would tell me stories about places and show me houses where people she knew lived. It was pretty magical to be given a song line that connected my Wiradjuri family to my Yuin family, from the Brungle Valley to Wallaga Lake, and all the places in between.

Nan told me many stories that I tell my grand-children at bedtime in Brungle. I am so proud to tell her story.

Nan now rests peacefully on the hill at Brungle cemetery watching over her family. She passed away at 92 and I sat with her the day she passed away for a few hours. I held her hand and I cried, her spirit had left, and her body remained. I know her spirit lives here with us, all of her family left behind, and for the generations to come.

Nan taught me so much. She told me to listen to my parents, listen to my old people, don't talk back, be respectful to everyone you meet and be considerate of other people. Yindyamarra was the way Nan lived her life, she loved life and she loved her family. This is my Wiradjuri story, a story of yindyamarra and ngurbul ♥

BRUNGLE CREEK

by Emma May Penrith
Born 24 May 1912
Passed 22 February 2005

Oh, how did you get your curious name?
O' Pretty Brungle creek.
Tell me too from whence you came,
I'd like to hear you speak.
The hills of high Tomorroma range,
join hands to swell your streams and to the valleys
green and sure,
you see the sunlight gleam.

The tribe of Aboriginals three hundred years ago
camped on your banks and sat at ease,
to watch your waters flow.
They bathed, they danced, they sung Bungle Bungle,
they chased kangaroos,
perhaps they called you Brungle Brungle.
I wonder if it's true,

you wonder slowly here and there
you wind now in and out,
amongst the gums that grow so fair,
and willows round about.
I often walk your banks,
to search for ferns and flowers,
at night the pixies play their pranks,
and fairies dance for hours.

Growing Up Wiradjuri Means Learning to Listen

Uncle Stan Grant Snr

When I was a little fellow growing up, I went to public school. Our principal there, we called him headmaster in those days, was John O'Brien. He was doing a class one day on Muruwari people. He said, 'We have here, written by a man,' he could have mentioned names of the author but anyway, he said that 'Wogga Wogga means the place of many crows.'

In the first place, it's not Wogga Wogga, and secondly, a place of many crows is not Wagga Wagga, it's Waggon Waggon. So I put my hand up.

He said, 'Yes, Stan, what can I do for you?'

'Sir, Wagga Wagga, or Wogga Wogga as you say, doesn't mean the place of many crows.'

'Oh, so what do you think it means?'

'It's not what I *think* it means, it's what I *know* it means. It's our language. It means the place of dance and celebration.'

'The book here tells me that it would be the place of many crows, so that's what we'll stick with, the place of many crows.'

He was more or less saying to me, 'You don't know what you're talking about.'

I knew what I was talking about, but the man who wrote this 'place of many crows' doesn't. And I understand how they got confused with it, because Wagga Wagga does sound a bit like Waggon Waggon, but it's not quite the same. If you say, 'Waggon, Waggon', you're saying then the place of many crows. Not a place, just many crows. And Wagga Wagga means dance celebration. So it's got nothing to do with crows at all, so I've got a real problem with this.

So this goes back to when I was about nine or ten years old, and it's been bugging me ever since that these people seem to think that Wagga is a place of many crows. They even got the pronunciation of the place wrong. It's not Wogga. It's Wagga, and Wagga Wagga means dancing, celebrating.

I went to the Wagga council and I explained this to them. They sort of ignored me. But the fact is, it's my language, our language, and I keep trying to tell them it's got nothing to do with crows whatsoever. It's got to do with dancing, celebrating. To say Wagga means dance. To say Wagga Wagga means dancing and celebrating, having a good time. I thought the council were going to change it, but they've not done that so far. Probably it's been over a year since I've spoken to them. But when I started this conversation, I knew it would take a long, long time to change it.

I was watching the TV the other day, and they were filming the Wagga council, and I saw a big crow sitting in the middle of the announcement, so obviously they're still happy with their crows. If they want to stay with the crows then that's okay. I'm not bitter about it, but I still think it should be changed. I've been saying this for a long time, and it's going to be a lot longer yet too. I hope they do change it before I kick the bucket. When I pass on to the next great hunting ground in the sky, well maybe they'll change it then.

There's also another place out here where they're doing some artwork on the silo down at a little place near Lockhart called Milbrulong. They say that Milbrulong means rosellas. I don't know what Milbrulong means. There's no Milbrulong in our language, as far as I know. Wilbegan is the word for rosellas, that's another thing they mixed up. They don't hear what we hear. They don't hear the sounds we know in our language.

When you learn a language, you have to listen to the sounds. Our sound is not like English. For example, there's no R sound in our language, and the N-G is very hard to hear. Our language does sounds like N-G, A-Y, D-Y, we have very different sounds in our language. There are over 600 words in our language so far that we have starting with N-G.

It's really important that you listen closely to what people are saying. Now if a person said, 'Look out there. What do you see?'

I said, 'I see a tree.'

'Is that all you see?'

No. A tree has many functions. If you see a tree there, there's water somewhere. A tree needs water somewhere with that. You have to be out there, wait for it, but it's there. And if you want protection, the tree will give you protection. You can use the bark for building up a little shack or something, a little gunyah, a wurley, whatever you want to call it.

And the leaves of there, there are seeds on the leaves that you can feed the life. The moisture in the leaf will keep you living. The sap in that tree will also keep you living. There's a lot more to a tree than just a tree. If you say, 'I see a tree', there's a lot more there than what you see.

And listen and hear, the same thing. Look and see, listen and hear. My grandfather always said that, many, many times to me. 'Boy, you got to look, you got to see, and listen, and you got to hear.' That's the important issue of that, listening and hearing and looking and seeing. And when you look, you got to see a lot more than you're looking at. And when you listen, to hear a lot more than what the person is saying.

Listen to the background fact. Listen to what their words are saying, as she's saying them. Just listen to what they're actually saying, and learn to listen properly.

There's a lot of non-Indigenous people don't know how to listen, and our lot, we were taught to listen. You probably had the same thing when you were a little kid, too.

My grandfather would often say, 'Boy, you're not hearing me. Listen and hear what I'm saying to you.'

You've got to listen, and you've got to hear very closely.

Jimmy James

Uncle James Ingram

My name's James Ingram. I come from Wattle Hill. Wattle Hill's part of Leeton and Leeton is part of the Narrungdera clan area of the great nation of Wiradjuri. I spent my early days on Wattle Hill. It was probably the happiest time of my life with my mum and dad, and brothers and sisters, and my grandmother and all my uncles and aunts and cousins. We were pretty happy up there.

One night they came and dragged us all out of our homes and bulldozed our homes in front of us and set them alight. Of course, everybody had to find somewhere else to live. We ended up out at Wamoon.

Everything was going all right there for a while and then Mum went away to pick asparagus and basically never come back. Dad tried his best, but the welfare came for us. My nan turned up and saved us. We ended up out at Stanbridge and stayed there through all my primary years and then we moved into town when I was a teenager. In between, all that time, my dad used to come and pick me up and take me out in the shearing sheds, and my grandfather, Uncle George, Uncle Frank and other relatives, and we used to stay out in the shearing sheds and camp out there for the duration of the contract. You'd get up at the crack of dawn. It was my job to get the fire lit and the billy on. Uncle George Ingram was my hero, he could shear 200 sheep in a day before 2pm and then sit back and laugh at the other men who were still going. And for me, it was never light work.

When we had time, we always checked out all the Wiradjuri sites that were around that my grandfather and my dad knew about. We'd do maintenance on them and make sure they were okay and all that sort of stuff. It's helped me later on in life to be able to do my care for

Country activities that I do because I've had that knowledge from Grandfather and Dad and my uncles.

I used to spend a lot of time with me nan and my aunties picking potatoes, peas, pumpkin and onions, you name it, we picked it. Oranges, lemons, grapefruits, grapes of course. I picked in and around Wamoon and Stanbridge. There wasn't much time to have a childhood. I started picking oranges when I was about eight years old and picked till I was about 15 or 16 years old. It was basically all about putting food on the table. It was hard work. It didn't hurt me, it taught me how to work later in life and the value, you know, of family, money and making it stretch as far as we could. I just wanted to help my grandmother out, help put food on the table, being the eldest.

When I wasn't picking fruit, I was chipping big weeds, thistles on rice farms. I was tractor driving a plough and I'd get on well with farmers cos I grew up with their kids. I still know some today.

I played rugby league in the winter months when I was about eight or nine. I played with the farmers' kids, so we worked and socialised together.

I couldn't get an apprenticeship as a carpenter when I was in high school so I went on to Year 12. I ended up in Sydney at Teacher's College. I did two years of a teaching degree, I guess, and realised that it wasn't for me and went off labouring.

I went back home and walked into the Leeton Commonwealth Employment Services and they said they had a job for me as a Vocational Officer, helping my people get jobs. I done that for about four years and loved every minute of it. I was tied up with a mob called Aboriginal Employment and Training Branch, great people. Then I ended up at the Wiradjuri Regional Lands Council. I was a Field Officer there and acting CEO for a while.

We used to go around and do all the community development for communities, especially housing. Part of what we did was making sure people got the right house that they wanted, not some bureaucratic one that was forced upon them. We designed their houses around what their needs were. We also developed some Aboriginal training programs where people actually got to build their homes. We used to torment some of the ministers for infrastructure programs for communities, like new sewerage systems, and parks and playground areas.

Then I went home to Leeton and realised Leeton was being left behind in terms of assets that the community had. I was there for four years, we got 16 homes and four flats and two office complexes and a motel for Leeton. Helped build up their profile and make sure Leeton got its fair share.

Then I moved back to Wagga and took up a job with Murrumbidgee Catchment Authority. That meant basically getting an investment strategy for people along the Murrumbidgee River where we all worked on the river and did our Cert IIs through to our Cert IVs in Land Management Conservation and Horticulture and all those sorts of things.

Out of the 20 people we had here in Wagga, 17 of them end up with permanent jobs. The program running Queanbeyan and Yass, Tumut, Wagga Wagga, Narrandera, Leeton, Darlington Point, Hay and Balranald so it was pretty good investment strategy and a pretty good capacity building program as well.

We also negotiated, along with Aunty Flo Grant, a Cultural Access Licence for people along the Murrumbidgee River. We're the only river that has that Cultural Access Licence.

I've just turned 60, I'm a cancer survivor and I'm married. We've been together on and off for the last 44 years. I'm semi-retired and I work for myself now and come and go as I please. I'm quite enjoying that. It's not so stressful anymore. Doing a bit of work with Visual Dreaming, doing some mentoring, and doing some work for some of the solar farms and other places, and helping our Wagga Wagga City Council wherever I can with their biodiversity strategies, caring for Country strategies and their walking track and all those things.

I look forward to mentoring young Wiradjuri peoples on Culture, heritage and caring for Country.

Out and About on Country

Aunty Mary Atkinson

I've got one sister, Violet, but my mum fostered over 100 kids in her time. She always used to say that the Lord blessed her with two children, but he blessed her also with all the others. She didn't foster them when she was young, but later in life, because their parents were in a bad place and couldn't be there for them. That's today too, you have kids in care for similar reasons. Mum's got a plaque down the main street of Wagga Wagga. I've got a big mob.

We travelled around when I was growing up. I was very young. I remember times as a child of eight years, Mum and Dad had to earn a living to be able to provide food and clothes and whatever for the families, so we travelled to wherever we could to pick fruit. Dad picked cherries and prunes, us kids just played around a bit, but we did pick the fruit from the bottom of the tree while everybody did their job. We went to Young for cherries and prunes and Griffith for the oranges. Then we went to Leeton for carrot, tomatoes, onions, and all that kind of stuff. I went to a lot of different schools which I didn't like, mainly because sometimes you'd be there without friends, without your family in a strange place.

As I grew up we travelled around more around the Riverina, the fruit bowl. There were always some family members there that I did play with. I remember Aunty Alice's kids, she married a Williams, and they used to live over in Brungle and we'd go there and stay in their little two-bedroom hut. All of us kids would stay asleep in one bed.

In all those places that we visited, we always had family out doing the same thing. I remember my grandfather and grandmother used to pick fruit too, and they'd be coming down in the horse and the cart. They'd say, 'Oh, Jackie and Mary, we're all going to get some nice fresh fruit or veggies to eat tonight'. Whatever we had, we all shared together because life was too hard back then. In Australia, a lot of things happen, but we are in a lucky country.

We'd go and we'd play because they had a lot of wide open spaces, beautiful country, and we used to go around picking up the tins and use it as a mouse catcher. I said I wouldn't do that, I'd be screaming!

We had little games to play. We used to play hopscotch, or play in the river. But we couldn't stay there too late. We were always told we couldn't be there after dark or someone would get us, and we believed all those stories. That's what they told us. They would share stories about things like the Bunyip.

But we'd go down there to the Yass River for hours and play on the rocks. We would build little cubby houses, have their little beds, little kitchens, cook our berries and plums and then make mud pies and all that stuff and go swimming in the river.

We used to play Eye Spy with My Little Eye, and a clapping hands game. I remember as a kid running around with no shoes on in the rain. Things like that were good. And we walked everywhere, not like today. We used to go and collect the drink bottles from the side of the road because we used to get five cents for collecting and get some money. We would spend the money on lollies and ice creams.

As I got older when I was 12, my uncle, Mum's brother, he used to live at Yass. So she said, 'Oh, you're getting a little bit older, so you need to stay with him'. So I stayed there and went to school at Yass High, and I stayed there with my uncle.

I didn't like that either, so I left school early, when I was 14, because back then they didn't have the support that they have now in schools. When I was 15, I moved to Sydney with my mum. I worked in the factory at PMU sauce. Ironically now, I'm working back in education and telling kids how important it is because it can take you a lot of places, get you a lot of places too.

We are resilient people in the way that we've survived. All the way through my life, Mum and Dad have always said you treat people right and they'll treat you right, which hasn't always been the case. For us as Aboriginal people we always lived on the outskirts of town. But we all stuck together and built up that resilience, and we have survived. That's what I tried to tell Martha my grandchild. I want to instil in them that nothing's given to you, you've got to work for it. All the way through my family, we've always fought for our rights and the wrongs that people have been through and helped people.

Even though it was sad times back then, we still made a good time out of it because we were family, we were all together, and we loved each other. Our cousins were our brothers and sisters. Even today we look at our cousins as our sisters or our brothers.

We go to a lot of funerals because that's what we're taught, to be respectful. We don't say 'that's not your cousin' or refer to anyone as a 'distant' cousin. That's a part of your family, part of your life, part of your heritage. So you've got to pay that respect to the people that are mourning. With coronavirus, we haven't had the chance. We've had that much sorry business in our community since the pandemic and we haven't had the chance to mourn with each other because there could only be ten people in a funeral.

We weren't scared of our Elders when we were young. A lot of people say they're scared. We weren't scared of them, we just knew what they said had to be respected and what they said they meant. So you knew that, and if you didn't do the right thing you knew there was going to be repercussions. I still respect my Elders because they've got to be listened to. You have the stories, they have the knowledge.

I've always been a positive person. I believe you should always look after your family because they're most important, especially children and the Elders. Just be the best you can and never be afraid of failure.

Sweet Memories

Aunty Isabel Reid

Hi, I'm Isabel Reid. I'm better known as Aunty Isabel. I'd like to let you know a little bit about my life, about growing up Wiradjuri.

My father's name was Alfred James Hampton. My mother was Florence Hickey and my grandparents were Thomas and Cora Hickey. Mum's people all came from Brungle. I'm only learning a little bit about my family now.

Mum and Dad travelled around a lot looking for work back in 1932. I was born just before the Great Depression or round about that time and things were pretty hard. I grew up in Quambone, New South

Wales, and travelled to Dubbo, that's where most of us grew up, around the Dubbo area.

We used to go to church across the road from where I lived. This was before I was taken away as a young girl. We were only little kids, about five or six years old.

We used to go to Sunday school every weekend. We'd love going there because we used to get these little text cards, little verses out of the bible, and we'd have to say them every time we came back to class next Sunday. I loved Sunday school. We'd come home and show our mothers all the little texts we'd gathered up. If we got about ten, we'd get a larger one, there'd be something longer written on that card and then we'd remember that and recite that one too.

I've still got a photo of all us kids around 1938. Some of them are grandparents now.

At Sunday school they taught us a little song. A chap by the name of Wesley Caddy. He was in the AIM, the Aboriginal Inland Mission Church, and they travelled around talking with all the Aboriginal people and the children back then. They were missionaries.

Wesley Caddy happened to be there in Dubbo at

this time at our church, he came there and he taught us this little song. I'm not sure what language it was, but I can still remember that day. I was only six or seven years old. I can still remember that. I haven't spoken about it or told anyone about it because I was a bit uneasy about the different language and because I was Wiradjuri, I thought that maybe we'd get into trouble because we were only little. So I kept that a secret. But if you'd like to hear it, I'll sing it to you now.

He sends the rainbow, the lovely rainbow.
He sends the rainbow with the rain.
He sends the sunshine, upon the shadow.
He sends the rainbow with the rain.

in Wiradjuri, the song goes

Abala bundenar
Ayureki yunda
Abala bundenar
Ayureki walla mullo

Abala bundenar
Ayureki yunda
Abala bundenar
Ayureki walla mullo

These were good times, but when I was seven, because of the NSW Act of Protection, I was taken away to the Cootamundra Aboriginal Girls Home and I grew up there. That was what the past government made sure happened with Aboriginal children. It was no fault of mine or no fault of my parents. They were good parents.

I live in Wagga Wagga now and I'm a grandmother. I came to Wagga Wagga with my husband and my children in the 1970s for better education and housing. I have six boys, five girls, and I've raised three grandchildren as well. I love what I'm doing now. I hope that later on in life our young people take a little bit of insight from what we're doing in life. We're doing the best we can for our young people, because they are our future and I think we need to focus on them.

Welcome to Country

Hi, it's me again, Aunty Isabel. I'd like to talk a little bit about why we do Welcome to Country and why it's so important.

Welcome to Country is a very important and necessary protocol for us to do, because this is our ancestors' Country. You mightn't want anyone to come onto your land without welcoming them or giving them permission – this is the same thing Aboriginal people did years ago. The new settlers came here, they tried to make out the land was theirs, but it was always Aboriginal land. It always will be Aboriginal land.

We are the caretakers of that land now and that's why it's important for us to make sure that people get welcomed to this land even if they lived here for many years. We must always respect that it is Aboriginal land.

We pay respects always when we go onto someone else's land, and we wouldn't go onto someone's land without getting their permission. It's the same with Aboriginal people and land. And that's why Welcome to Country is very important.

26 September 1957, Griffith

Uncle Norman Little

I was born in Griffith and reared by Nan and Pop. Growing up I moved around a lot, all over the place. I lived in Harden, Kingsvale, Wombat, as well as Wagga Wagga.

We used to play a few games when I was a kid. I used to play one called rounders with my cousins. It was half rounders half rugby league; we would play it in the back paddock in Kingsvale. Rounders is a game played like softball but not as many rules as softball. It's like softball with tackling, a lot of it. A lot more people on the paddock too, it wasn't like having anyone sitting off like you would sit on the bench, everyone got to be involved. The best part was playing in the paddock. It was a great game.

We used to play it with all the Littles, Murrays and the Brights, and it wasn't bad. In rounders, you stop people from getting home any way you can, as my sister Eve found out. She was running home, I went across and told her to stay and she didn't take any notice, so I tackled the back of her legs. We won the game 1-0, there weren't many getting home. We kept our best tacklers close to home base.

We also used to play tackle in the back of Uncle Arthur's house in Harden, Binalong Street, and by the end of the year there was hardly any fence left because we would tackle our mates through the fence.

The silly part about that was there was a football oval 200 yards away and we didn't go near it. We had seven a side, I reckon it was the first time seven a side was introduced. The two youngest had to get on each side and they were only allowed to tackle each other. But everything else was enter at your own risk.

We had to rebuild the fence as we tackled our cousins through it a few too many times. Uncle Arthur once threatened me with his whip and he whipped my cousin Alan Little first and I said to Alan ‘It won’t hurt for long’ and when Uncle Arthur heard that whilst he was walking away, he called me back and said ‘Where are you going Norman?’ and whipped me next and then Alan said to me ‘Now see, it won’t hurt for long Norman’.

Uncle Arthur was pretty deadly with that whip, he whipped me on my arse, I think it took a bit of skin off.

We had one black and white television, but there were better things to do than sit in front of a television all day. We would go out and work picking cherries, prunes and apples, whatever fruit was in season. And we used to pick before we went to school and then after school get off the bus and continue picking until it got dark.

Author Biographies

Anita Heiss is a proud Wiradjuri woman who was born on Gadigal Country and spent much of her life on Dharawal land near La Perouse. She is one of Australia's most prolific and well-known authors, publishing across genres including non-fiction, historical fiction, commercial fiction and children's novels.

Aunty Lorraine Tye is a weaver, artist, storyteller and researcher living in Wagga Wagga. She has made significant contributions to the reclamation of Wiradjuri cultural practices through her art and creative practices.

Aunty Elaine Lomas was born in Griffith, NSW, and currently lives in Canberra. Her Ancestral Lands and Cultural connections are between the Marrambidya (Murranbidgee), Galari (Lachlan), Wambuul (Macquarie) and Castlereagh rivers. Elaine is a speaker and teacher of Wiradjuri language, and an Associate Lecturer in Wiradjuri Language, Culture and Heritage.

Aunty Cheryl Penrith is a Wiradjuri woman who also has cultural connection to the Yuin and Wotjoboluk nations. A mother and a nanny of five, she comes from a large, proud strong family. She lives in Wagga Wagga and is originally from Brungle and Tumut.

Uncle Stan Grant Senior AM lives in Wagga Wagga. He has worked tirelessly for decades to revive and preserve the Wiradjuri language for future generations. He is a writer, a researcher and a teacher.

Uncle James Ingram grew up in Leeton and has lived in Wagga Wagga for 40 years. He holds knowledge in cultural burnings, traditional tools, land ownership, land use planning, water ways, land rights and agriculture.

Aunty Mary Atkinson is a Wiradjuri/Ngunnawal woman and has a great passion for family and cultural connections. She enjoys watching her grandchildren play football, touch footy and netball, and her rugby team is the Parramatta Eels. She has a large family with connections to Merritt, Carrol, Charles and McGuiness families.

Aunty Isabel Reid is one of the oldest living survivors of the Stolen Generations. Born in 1932, she was abducted on her way home from school and taken from her family to Cootamundra. She now lives in Wagga Wagga and was named senior Australian of the Year in 2021.

Uncle Norman Little was born in Griffith and grew up in Harden, Young and Wagga Wagga. He was part of the Waagan Waagan Aboriginal men's group, focused on promoting awareness of conservation and land management for Aboriginal sites around Wagga. He now enjoys watching his grandchildren play sport and socialising with family and friends.

Also from Magabala Books...

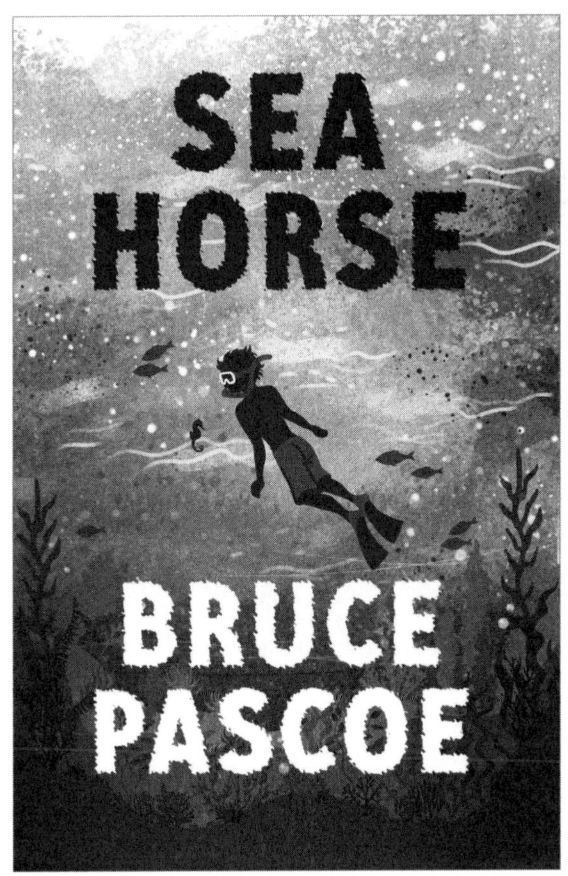

Open Your Heart to
Country
JASMINE SEYMOUR

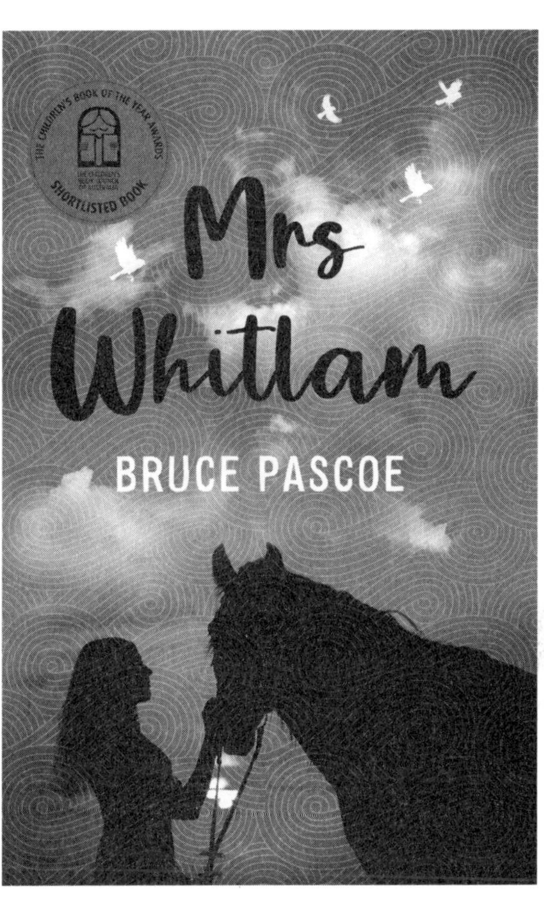
THE CHILDREN'S BOOK OF THE YEAR AWARDS
SHORTLISTED BOOK
Mrs Whitlam
BRUCE PASCOE

The
Shop Train
Josie Wowolla Boyle
illustrated by Paul Seden

US
MOB
WALAWURRU
DAVID SPILLMAN
& LISA WILYUKA

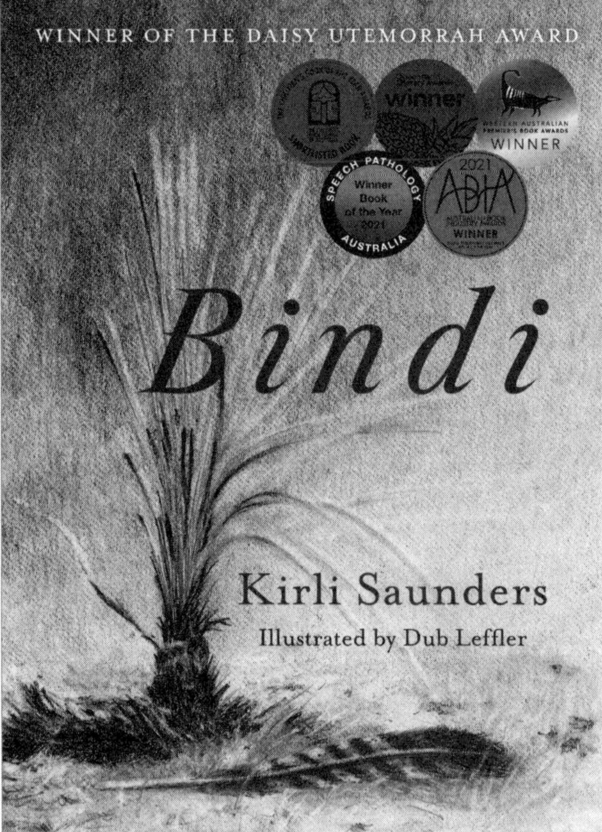
WINNER OF THE DAISY UTEMORRAH AWARD
WINNER
WESTERN AUSTRALIAN PREMIER'S BOOK AWARDS
WINNER
SPEECH PATHOLOGY
Winner
Book
of the Year
2021
AUSTRALIA
2021
ADIA
WINNER
Bindi
Kirli Saunders
Illustrated by Dub Leffler

HONOUR BOOK
finalist
2019
ABIA
SHORTLISTED
SPEECH PATHOLOGY
Shortlisted
Book
of the Year
AUSTRALIA
black
cockatoo
Carl Merrison and Hakea Hustler